Usborne Fairytale Sticker Stories

Sleeping Beauty

Illustrated by Stephen Cartwright

Retold by Heather Amery and Laura Howell

How to use this book

This book tells the story of Sleeping Beauty.
Some words in the story have been replaced by pictures.
Find the stickers that match these pictures and stick them over the top.
Each sticker has the word with it to help you read the story.

Some of the big pictures have pieces missing.
Find the stickers with the missing pieces to finish the pictures.

A yellow duck is hidden in every picture. When you have found
the duck you can put a ⬤ sticker on the page.

Once there was a good King and Queen.

After many years, the  had a baby

girl. The  and Queen were delighted,

and loved the little Princess very much.

2

The baby Princess was christened.

Six good  came to a feast at the

royal palace. But the  forgot to ask

the seventh fairy, who was cruel and wicked.

Five of the fairies made good wishes.

The sixth  was about to make

her wish for the little . Suddenly

the wicked fairy appeared, looking very angry.

"The Princess will die," she said.

"She'll prick her on a spinning wheel."

"No," said the good . "I wish that

she won't die, but will sleep for a hundred years."

5

The Queen cried and the King shouted.

"All spinning wheels in my kingdom must

be burned," said the  . "Then the

Princess will never prick her on one."

6

The Princess grew up in the palace.

When she was seventeen, she had a Grand

Birthday Ball. The good  came to

the Ball. They had all forgotten the .

7

Next day, the Princess found a staircase.

It led to a little room she had never seen before.

Inside was an old woman with a  .

It was the  in disguise.

wicked fairy

Princess

fairies

finger

I found the duck!

I found the duck!

I found the duck!

fairy

I found the duck!

Queen

guards

old man

doors

I found the duck!

I found the duck!

palace

forest

fairies

Princess

King

Prince

Princess

bed

Princess

Queen

I found the duck!

I found the duck!

I found the duck!

fairy

baby

King

I found the duck!

finger

spinning wheel

I found the duck!

King

I found the duck!

I found the duck!

I found the duck!

Prince

King

fairies

I found the duck!

I found the duck!

wicked fairy

hand

"What are you doing?" said the Princess.

"I'm spinning, my dear. Come closer, and I'll

show you," said the old woman. The

put out her  and pricked her finger.

9

At once, she fell fast asleep.

Everyone else in the  went to sleep

too. The six good fairies carried the Princess to

her  . The wicked fairy vanished.

Nothing moved in the palace.

Everything was still and silent for a hundred

years. A thick 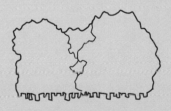 grew around the

palace. The good  watched over it.

11

One day, a young Prince came by.

He saw the roof of the palace and asked an old

man about it. "A  sleeps in there,"

said the  , "but there's no way in."

12

The Prince walked to the palace.

The trees moved apart and let him through. He

ran past the sleeping  , up the steps

and through the  . It was very quiet.

13

He found the Princess fast asleep.

She was so beautiful, he kissed her gently. The

 opened her eyes and smiled. "At last,

a handsome  to save me," she said.

Everyone in the palace woke up.

"I'm hungry," said the . "Tonight

we'll have a great feast," and she thanked the

for saving everyone.

15

The Prince wanted to marry the Princess.

"Of course," said the  . The Prince and

got married, and were very happy.

Cover design by Michael Hill   Digital manipulation by Keith Furnival and Leonard Le Rolland

First published in 2006 by Usborne Publishing Ltd, Usborne House, 83-85 Saffron Hill, London EC1N 8RT, England. www.usborne.com

Copyright © 2006 Usborne Publishing Ltd. The name Usborne and the devices ♔ ⊕ are Trade Marks of Usborne Publishing Ltd. All rights reserved.
No part of this publication may be reproduced, stored in a retrieval system, or transmitted in any form or by any means, electronic, mechanical,
photocopying, recording or otherwise without the prior permission of the publisher. First published in America in 2006. U.E. Printed in Malaysia.